QUEEN
SARDINE

A TEMPLAR BOOK

First published in the UK in 2014 by Templar Publishing,

an imprint of The Templar Company Limited,

Deepdene Lodge, Deepdene Avenue, Dorking, Surrey,

RH5 4AT, UK

www.templarco.co.uk

ISBN 978-1-84877-420-9

Printed and bound by CPI Group (UK) Ltd, Croydon, CR0 4YY

QUEEN SARDINE

Kate Willis-Crowley

templar

For Alfie and his cat-crazy friends!

A SOGGY MOGGY

I love cats. I can't have a pet, though. Mum says it's a big enough job looking after the two of us, let alone anything with fur or feathers.

She did get me a fish once, when I was really little, but I only had him a day. I put him in the bath with me and he started swimming funny, then he died. Kind of put me off having fish. It put me off having baths too. Mum says I've got to have a bath every other morning, even when I'm already all clean and fresh-smelling. That's just the rule. So here I am, in the bath. Again.

I'm making a massive bubble bath beard. It's a good one. One minute I'm like this:

Then suddenly there's a

CRASH... SPLASH...

MEEeeoooooOWww...

and I'm like this:

Because a big, fat stripy cat hurls itself
through the open window, into my bath.
It splash lands next to me, then scrambles
out at lightning speed.

I scream, and straight away, I wish
I hadn't, because:

1. I swallow most of my beard.
2. The cat looks even more scared than
   I am.

It looks me straight in the eyes and hisses, "*Help me!*"

No joke. Proper words.

At first, I'm just too flabbergasted to speak. I mean… **Wowzers!** A talking cat! And then, when I *do* speak, the words get all mushed together, "W-w-whaddidoosay?"

"Please! *Please* help me," it begs.

"But… cats can't talk!" I croak, still gobsmacked.

"Neither can you, it seems," the cat says. It slinks back a little, looking wary, and glances up at the window, like maybe it's made a mistake.

"Look, you *are* Ivy Meadows, aren't you?" it asks.

I nod.

"Then *please* help me! You must! I've heard about you. You're kind to cats. That's what he said!"

"Who said?" I ask.

"Never mind that, just say you'll help!" it urges.

I nod again. "Okay…" I whisper, not really sure what I'm agreeing to.

"Thank you. *Thank you*, kind girl," the cat whispers back.

I grab a couple of towels and climb out of the tub.

As the cat dries off, I'm sure it looks
familiar.

"Aren't you Mr and Mrs Trott's cat?"
I ask.

Mr and Mrs Trott moved into a house
across the road a few weeks ago. Mr Trott
is big, grumpy and grunts instead of

talking. Mrs Trott is all buffed and plucked and polished and she talks *all the time*. I've seen a cat – *this* cat, I think – looking out of their front window. And I've heard Mrs Trott calling, in her sing-songy voice,

"Saardi-i-i-i-i-i-ine! Sardeeny-weeeeeeenykins!"

I stroke the cat's damp fur. It looks a bit annoyed – have I said something wrong?

"You're Sardine, right?"

"I'm *Queen* Sardine. At least, I used to be queen of my old home. *He* says I'll soon be queen of Kipper Street and

Cuttle Street too, and maybe that alley round the corner as well…"

"Crab Alley?"

"Yes, that too," she sighs. "Queen of all of it!"

I start to ask again who *he* is, but she's not finished.

"And no one *owns* a queen! Yes, I *live* with Mr and Mrs Trott. They serve me…" She says this bit really slowly as though she's talking to someone a bit thick. "Except… except…" her ears flatten, like she's in danger.

"Except what?" I whisper.

"*Except they've gone mad!*" she hisses.

"They've let a *monster* live in our precious new home!"

What? No way! A monster on Kipper Street?

"What kind of monster?" I ask, a little bit scared of what the answer will be.

Queen Sardine looks at me with huge, wild eyes, "The *worst* kind of monster...

A fang-gnashing...
rip-snarling...
yip-yooowwlling...

grizzle-bristling...
fuzz-frizzling...

belly-burping...

stonk-stinking...

slobbersome mOnster!

And worst of all…

IT STEALS MY DINNERS!"

Poor Queen Sardine. Her ears are quivering and she starts mewing pitifully.

"Oh… oh dear," I say. "Please don't get upset, Queen Sar—"

"*Your Majesty*," whimpers the soggy moggy. "Call me Your Majesty."

I hold in a giggle. "Er… all right… So, what are you going to do about this monster, *Your Majesty*?"

Queen Sardine rubs against my knees. "Well, I can hardly go back home. You'll look after me, I know you will," she purrs.

Gulp. I'm sure Mum doesn't want a cat, but Queen Sardine seems to have it all planned…

"Now, listen carefully," she says, "I will need somewhere ever so cosy to sleep…"

"I don't think Mum will let—" I begin.

"Don't interrupt!" says Queen Sardine. "I was just about to tell you about mealtimes. Twice a day, and plenty of snacks in between. Got that, little human?"

"My name's Ivy. But—"

"Fish is best, but chicken will do," she continues. "Oh, and you *must* remember to leave the bathroom window open so I can... so I can... *do my business*... if you know what I mean!"

I *do* know what she means.

This really isn't a good idea.

"I don't think Mum will—"

"Ah, now, I think it's best you don't tell your mum about me just yet," interrupts

Queen Sardine, "I don't think she'd understand me like *you* do, do you?"

"I doubt it," I say.

"So we're agreed then. I'll live here instead. Splendid. Right, I think I'm ready for some breakfast now," she purrs. "Something fishy perhaps?"

I don't remember actually agreeing to her *moving in*. I have a bad feeling about this. But she really *does* seem to need my help, and this might be my chance to have a pet…

Okay. First things first. I'll have to sneak Queen Sardine back to my bedroom.

"You *must* stay totally quiet and still," I whisper. Then I pick her up and lift her onto my head. I put a towel over her and tuck in the edges, so it looks like I've just wrapped up my wet hair. Kind of.

"Are you sure this is really necessary?" she grumbles.

"*Shh!*" I say, and I peep around the bathroom door. I tiptoe past the kitchen, then past the living room.

Mum's doing the ironing, so she's got the telly up loud.

"*Nearly there! I think we're safe...*" I whisper.

"Ivy?"

Think again.

"Er... Mum?"

She comes out with a humungous pile of my freshly ironed clothes. Queen Sardine stiffens on my head.

"Here. Can you manage? These need putting away."

I take the pile, which is so massive I can't see a thing over the top.

I turn to go, but she stops me.

"Wait," she says, "is that my towel?"

Oh crackers… "Maybe," I say, backing away down the hall. Queen Sardine is now frantically clawing my scalp.

YeeoOOUch! I try hard not to wince.

"Well, it looks like it needs a wash," says Mum. "What's that on it? Fluff or hair or—"

Or fur…

"Yeah… fluff! I'll stick it in the wash later," I call, further down the hall now and nearly at my bedroom door.

By this point, Queen Sardine has knotted my hair into a big bird's-nest clump with her claws.

Mum heads back to the ironing and I shuffle into my bedroom.

I dump the pile of clothes on the floor, close the door and try to lift Her Majesty off my head.

"*Ow-ow-ow!*" I cry, as I untangle her claws from my hair.

Queen Sardine isn't happy either. She jumps onto the bed and licks her paws, looking ruffled and grouchy. Great. My head's scratched to pieces and *she's* the one being grumpy.

"Here," I say, "cuddle Felina," and I put my *number-one-best-toy-ever* next to the pouting cat.

Made from Granny Mo's old curtains

Made from Granny Mo's old pyjamas

Made from Granny Mo's old bloomers (big knickers)

She sniffs my rag rabbit and bops it a bit with her paw. Then she nuzzles her head against Felina and stretches out on top of her, finally starting to relax.

Felina (full name: Felina Belina Daisy Flower) was handmade by Granny Mo, the lady who lives in the flat above us.

She's not really my granny, but she's got loads of grandkids so everyone calls her Granny Mo.

She gave me Felina when I was born and I secretly love her best of all my toys, even though I'm eight.

Queen Sardine seems to love her too.

"That's better," she says with a lazy smile. "Now, where's my fish?"

SOMETHING FISHY

Yuck, I hate fish. I hate *eating* fish, that is. Wouldn't mind another pet goldfish, although I'd have to promise Mum not to put it in the bath this time…

Anyway, I look through all the kitchen cupboards and find an old tin of tuna, but no tin-opener. Tucked behind the tuna is a jar of fish paste. That'll do. It's not big but maybe I can make sandwiches with it, make it go further.

I'm being as quick as I can. Bread, spread, chop. Bread, spread, chop. But just as I'm finishing, Mum walks in. She crosses the room to the fridge. Any minute now she'll turn around and see the sandwiches, and she'll start asking questions. Argh. At least Queen Sardine is hidden away safely in my bedroom.

"*Psst!*"

Great. Queen Sardine is now peeping round the kitchen door, right beside me.

"*Less bread, more fish!*" she hisses.

Mum looks over. "Did you say something?" she asks.

I quickly shake my head and lean in to hide the fish paste but it's too late, she's seen it.

"Ivy… you hate fish paste!"

"Oh. Yes! I *usually* hate fish paste, but… I… I thought I might try it again," I say.

There's no way she'll believe *that*, I think to myself, but apparently she does.

Mum points at the wobbling pile of sandwiches. "Couldn't you just try a little bit first?"

She laughs, shaking her head and turning to grab the milk from the fridge.

Next thing I know, my ankle's being clawed. YeeeOWZers! I bend down to rub it and see Queen Sardine under the kitchen table, looking worried.

"No! Don't listen to her! Keep going. Finish the jar!" she says.

I give the cat a glare and mouth back, "Go!"

"Ivy?" says Mum, and I stand up too fast, bopping my head on the table.

Mum doesn't even notice. She's looking in the cupboards for some glasses. Then she glances over.

"You've made quite a lot of sandwiches already. Maybe you should stop now," she says, before heading right over to me and sitting down at the table.

I pick up the plate of sandwiches and try to leave the kitchen.

"Hold it there, young lady!" says Mum. She starts to pour me a glass of milk.

I tell her, "It's okay, I'm not thirsty…"

But she says, "I've hardly seen you all morning. Stay and chat to me."

So I don't have much choice.

Gulp. I'll have to eat those stinky sandwiches.

Fishy pongy   Whiffy whiff

I sneak a peek under the kitchen table. At least Queen Sardine seems to have disappeared back to my bedroom.

Okay. Here goes.

I pick up the milk and sip slowly. If I take *forever* perhaps I can put off eating the fishy yuck.

Then Mum says, "Go ahead, eat up."

I pick up a sandwich. Oh, the smell…

I hold my breath and nibble one corner. Bleh. I'd rather eat slugs.

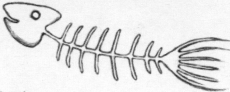

"It's… very nice," I lie.

The pile in front of me is humungous. At least a hundred more nibbles to go. I put the sandwich back to my lips.

Then, just as I'm about to bite down…

BRING BRING!! BRING BRING!!

Saved!

Mum jumps up.

"Sorry, lovey, I'd better get the phone," she says, and dashes out of the kitchen.

Queen Sardine lands on my lap with a sudden **KERFLUMP** and digs in her claws.

"Have you quite finished gobbling my

sandwiches?" she asks, pushing her head up to table level.

Sheesh. It's not like I *want* to be eating her food.

"Now, quick – move aside!" she says, and she grabs a sandwich in her mouth. "*Bwing de west!*" she mumbles, and dashes back to my room.

I grab the plate and my glass of milk, and follow her.

Back in my bedroom, Queen Sardine is ripping the bread apart and licking off the fish paste. Her ears prick up when I walk in.

"Oh, milk! Wonderful!" she grins.

I don't mind sharing.

"You're welcome to have some," she says, as she slurps it down. "Of course, *cream* would have been better, but I imagine you've done your best."

Charming.

"I'll try to remember that next time, Your Majesty," I say. I can't help smiling, though. Even when she's rude, she's kind of funny.

I give her the rest of the sandwiches. Queen Sardine licks and purrs, licks and purrs. Then she finds the only sunny spot on the windowsill, among my old teddies, and curls up in a little ball.

"Delicious food and a lovely place to catnap... Almost perfect," she says.

"Almost?" I ask.

Queen Sardine stretches a paw towards Felina, and I *very* kindly put my number-one-favourite toy next to her *again*.

"Perfect," she yawns.

Her eyes close, her head lolls and pretty soon, all I can hear is the **thrum thrum purrrrrrrrrrrr** of a sleeping cat with a very full tummy.

CAT OUT OF THE BAG

This afternoon, Mum and I are weeding the front garden. I don't like leaving Queen Sardine on her own, but my bedroom door is ajar and I've opened the bathroom window (in case she needs to *do her business*), so I guess she'll be okay.

Hopefully…

"You all right, honeybun?" Mum asks. She's got mud on her nose. I nod and try not to look like I'm worrying about the neighbours' cat... the neighbours who, right now, happen to be leaning on our gate. Oh great.

"Afternoo-hoon!" sings Mrs Trott. "Oooh, we were just saying how *we* should do a little bit of gardening, eh, Boris? Hmm? Bozzykins?"

"Huh! *We*..." snorts Mr Trott, "means *me*."

"Well well, who's a grumpy, lazy little Boris today then?" laughs Mrs Trott.

And Mr Trott grunts something that sounds like, "No bloomin' sleep... Bloomin' beast."

Beast. He definitely said *beast*.

Mrs Trott tuts and rolls her eyes, "Oh don't exaggerate, darling, you were snoring away all night long."

Then he starts grumbling, "Hmph… not *me* snoring… Bristly, drooling brute… Big old honking nose… Dirty claws… Don't know why I put up with it."

And after that, I know Queen Sardine really *was* telling the truth.

Mr Trott sort of shakes his head at us instead of saying goodbye, then he plods off down the road.

Mrs Trott stays behind to chit-chat with Mum. She's a bit *tra la la happy happy bouncy bouncy* but other than that, Mrs Trott is pretty normal. I mean, she definitely doesn't seem crazy enough to live with some drooling monster. But then, *I* couldn't live in a house with

Mr Trott and *she* seems to really like him. People can be weird.

I start bagging up the weeds. It feels a bit like I've kidnapped her cat — which I definitely *have not* — but I still feel guilty.

Oh great. To make matters worse, guess who else is outside today? Fabian Dodd.

Fabian lives at number seven with his mum, dad and gran. Everyone loves Fabian, but he's mean. *Really* mean.

He's just good at hiding it. And right now, he's cycling up and down the road, doing wheelies and jumping the kerb, and pulling nasty faces at me when no one else is looking.

But I've got more important stuff to

worry about. Mrs Trott keeps talking and talking and I think Mum's trying to get away, but she needs to try a bit harder.

Come on, Mum – I'm really starting to stress out. Queen Sardine has been on her own for hours…

Eventually, after a couple of squillion years, Mrs Trott says, "Toodle-pip," and heads home after Bozzykins.

Mum gives me a half-smile, but doesn't say anything about Mr and Mrs Trott, which means she thinks they're a bit odd, but she's too nice to say so. Instead, she just says, "Okay. That'll do for now."

Finally. We shake the mud off our shoes

and I follow Mum back indoors.

Of course, the first thing I want to do is check on Queen Sardine. But just as I'm about to go into my room, Mum turns back to me.

"Oh, I almost forgot!" she says. "You left the bathroom window open earlier. You *must* remember to close it, Ivy."

Uh-oh. My heart skips a few beats. "Did *you* close it?" I ask.

And she says, "Yes, darling, don't worry. Just be more careful in future."

"Right," I say, trying to sound normal.

I watch her disappear into the living room, telling myself to *act calm*. Then,

when she's out of sight, I dash into my bedroom. Seconds later, I find poor Queen Sardine pacing up and down, round and round.

"*I need to do my business!*" she howls. "You said you'd leave the window open. You promised!"

"I'm sorry! Mum closed it. I didn't know."

"I need to go outside *NOW*!" she says.

"Right... right..."

I look about desperately. "Here! Climb inside my school bag, I'll sneak you out."

We can't risk going to the bathroom because we'd have to pass by the living room. Mum might come out and start asking questions.

"What on earth have you got in there?"

"Why do you need your school bag in the bathroom?"

No. Too dangerous. I'll just have to sneak Queen Sardine out of the front door – it's right by my bedroom, after all.

Queen Sardine doesn't like this idea. She tells me that all this hiding in towels and bags is unqueenly. But she really *does* need to get outside, and fast, so she scrambles into the bag.

Quietly, we sneak out into the hall and to the front door. Mum's singing along to an advert on the TV. Perfect. She'll never hear me over the telly. I ease the front door open.

"Hello, Ivykins!" I nearly jump out of my skin. Because standing there, on the other side of the door, is Mrs Trott.

"I was about to knock," she explains.

"Oh…" I say. My school bag is wriggling on my back.

Mrs Trott doesn't notice. "I'm just wondering if you've seen our cat, Sardine. She hasn't come home for din-dins yet *and* she missed her brekkie. We're just a bit worried. She's a tabby cat, very cuddlesome. I don't suppose you've seen—"

"No! No... I haven't seen her," I say.

Queen Sardine wriggles some more and claws jab through the bag and into my waist.

"Ow! I mean... *H–Ow* about trying further down the road?" My eyes are watering as I squeeze out the words, "Good luck!" and even though I think she

52

wants to keep talking, I wave goodbye and close the door feeling very guilty.

"*What are you doing?*" hisses the bag on my back. "*I need to go out now! Now!*"

I can see through the spyhole that Mrs Trott has gone. The coast is finally clear. But as I reach for the latch, I hear a cough behind me and I know it's too late. I turn around and, just as I thought, Mum's in the hall, arms folded, looking unimpressed.

"What's in the bag, Ivy?" she says, in her serious *you're-in-big-trouble-young-lady* voice.

I lower the wriggling bag to the ground and turn around, very slowly, giving myself more thinking time.

"School stuff… my PE kit, ready for Monday morning," I say.

"And why is your PE kit moving?" Mum asks.

Busted.

I stare at the floor. The bag keeps wriggling. I sigh and whisper, "Sorry," (though I'm not sure if I'm saying sorry to Mum or to Queen Sardine…) and I open the bag. Queen Sardine shoots out in a panic. She sees Mum's pot plant in the corner of the hall. She makes a dash for it, leaps in and does a very long royal wee.

TROUBLE

Mum has one of her frowns on, which spells trouble. She opens the front door and Queen Sardine struts out, whiskers held high. But when Her Majesty looks back at me, I can tell she's embarrassed. She's just trying her best to hide it.

"You lied to Mrs Trott. And I suppose you've been lying to me all day," says Mum.

"Sorry," I sniff.

"But *why*, Ivy? Why would you take somebody else's cat?"

Whoa! What? Take her? No way. Not fair. I can feel my eyes stinging and going hot, which means I'm probably going to cry.

Oh bogies. When I cry, I can't get my words out properly and I end up honking like an out of breath donkey. But I have to say *something*, and anyway, I'm fed up with lying and secrets. So I take a deep breath and try not to honk too much.

"I… didn't!" I splutter. "She… came to me… for help – **honk** – and she's not just any c-c-cat… She's – **honk** – a queen!"

And with lots of snotty croaks and crazy honks, I tell Mum everything. All of it. The talking tabby cat…

... the fish
paste...

...the mOnster!

Mum puffs up her cheeks and breathes out really slowly.

"You've got a pretty wild imagination," she says, and screws up her eyes. "I don't like you telling me these crazy stories.

If you were worried about the cat, why didn't you just say?"

I shrug.

"Sorry."

I knew Mum would never believe me. No point going on about it.

"Poor Mr and Mrs Trott will be worried sick!"

"Sorry, Mum," I say. Again.

"Well, I should walk you straight over to the Trotts'. It's *them* you need to say sorry to."

Gulp.

Not the Trotts' house. What if the monster's there?

Mum stares into space. She's thinking.

"This is so *unlike* you, Ivy. You must really care for that cat…" she says.

Hang on. Am I going to get away with this?

"Just this once," she says.

Huh? I wait. Mum's nostrils bulge as she sighs through her nose.

"Just this once I'll sort it out. I'll phone the Trotts. I'll say I saw Sardine in the garden or something."

Phew. "Thanks, Mum," I say.

"I'm still not happy about you lying to me," she says.

"I know. Sorry."

Mum's nostrils bulge again. "Okay. Enough *sorrys* for now. Go and wash the mud off your hands while I get this over with."

I dawdle. From the hallway I can hear little bits of Mum's phone call to Mrs Trott.

"Yes, that's right, in our front garden… back home already? Fantastic. No, no bother at all… What's that? No, I missed it… Sally's secretly married to Dan's cousin's dog's vet? She never is!"

When she starts chatting about telly I stop listening. I slump back to the bathroom and look at my puffy eyes in the mirror. I feel like I might start crying again. Yes, I'm *really* happy about not being in trouble any more. But it's not that simple. Queen Sardine, my new best friend, is back with the monster again. Maybe she's being slobbered on and chewed at this very *moment*…

Except, she isn't.

SCRATCH, SCRATCH.

She's at the bathroom window. Pressed up against the glass, staring at me.

"Your Majesty!"

My heart's thudding. I know I shouldn't, but I open the window and let Queen Sardine in. Then, holding my finger to my lips, I close the bathroom door and turn on the taps at the sink, so Mum won't hear us talking.

"I thought you'd gone back to your people?" I whisper, as loudly as I can.

"Oh, for goodness sake!" She rolls her eyes at me. "I thought I'd explained all this to you! There's a monster living with my people. I went by quickly to check up on them, and… well, I ate a quick meal there, just to be polite… but I can't *stay* there! I must say, you've got an appalling memory, even for a human."

I ignore that last bit. "So, where are you going to sleep tonight, Your High—"

"Shush, don't fuss. I dare say I'll think of something. That's not why I'm here," she interrupts. "I'm *here* because you said you'd help and obviously, it'll have to be more than just the two of us. A small army, perhaps… It'll take some planning… We'll meet tomorrow morning to work it all out. After breakfast. Your front garden."

"Wait! Hold on, Your Majesty. I don't know what you're talking about. A small army? To do what?" I ask.

"Oh, will you *please* pay attention!" Queen Sardine groans at me. "Now listen hard and I'll go very slowly."

I cross my arms and wait. "Go on, Your Majesty. I'm listening."

"I'm *here* because tomorrow… *Tomorrow we fight the monster!*"

FIGHT DAY

Next morning, I wake up hot and sweaty.

I'd been dreaming I was a knight in armour. Something was following me, growling and licking its lips, but my helmet was so massive and heavy on my head that I couldn't see a thing. I'd started swinging my sword about, hoping I'd get lucky and **thwack** the monster, but it just got closer and growlier, until I could feel

its hot breath on my face. Then my alarm
clock went off.

For a split second I'm relieved. It was
just a dream… But then I remember –
today is fight day.

What had Queen Sardine said? After breakfast? My clock says it's almost eight. Time to drag myself out of bed.

Mum is already up, sipping coffee and doing a crossword puzzle at the kitchen table.

"Help me, sweetheart," she yawns, pointing at her puzzle, "a word that means *savage beast*. Seven letters… *m*, something, *n*, something, *t*, something, *r*…"

Hmph. I know the answer to *that* one straight away. "Monster."

"Monster! Of course! Wonderful."

Yeah. Sure. Wonderful. Unless you've got to fight one.

I'm going to be
late, so I hoover down
a big mouthful of juice
and a tiny bowl of cereal and ask if I can
play outside.

Mum looks up. She's got
pen on her nose. "Brush
teeth, brush hair... and
you do know you're still
in your pyjamas, don't
you?" she laughs.

Oh. Good point.

Five minutes
later, I'm ready
to go.

I'm lucky. Most of the kids in my class don't get to play outside, but my mum doesn't mind. Mostly, it's because everybody knows everybody on Kipper Street, so there's always someone to tell on me if I break the rules.

The rules are:

1. Stay out of the road (unless you're crossing it, obviously).

2. Don't go past the post box (the bottom of Kipper Street).

3. Don't talk to strangers (I once said to Mum, "What if the stranger is a little kid who's lost with a broken leg?" and Mum said in that case I should use my common sense. I said that if I've got common sense then why do I have to have rules? She pulled a *don't-push-your-luck* face. But I think I had a good point.).

Anyway, I shout, "Bye," and step out of the front door. It's blazing hot outside, and Granny Mo's window is open in the flat above. She's got the radio on. It's warbling and wafting out into the garden along with the smell of fresh bread.

Granny Mo sees me and calls out, "Want some?" For maybe the first time ever, I'm too nervous to eat.

My breakfast is already churning in my tummy. So, I shake my head.

"No? Well that's not like Ivy Meadows. Mus' be some imposter!"

She's nice, Granny Mo.

"Come see me when your belly wakes up," she calls, and she goes back to her baking.

I notice Queen Sardine is already here, in the front garden, stretched across Mum's flower bed. When she gets up, she leaves a flat patch of pansies. I wonder if she's been there all night. She struts over to me straight away and rubs against my ankle.

"So lovely to see you," she says. "You're a bit late, but never mind. Let's get down to business."

I crouch beside her and wait to hear her grand plan.

"Now, I've been thinking," she begins, "and I *may* know someone who *might* be able to help us. *If* we can find him."

"You do? So he's fought monsters before?" I ask.

"Oh, very probably," she says.

"So, who is he, Your Majesty?"

"I'm sure you must know him — *he* knows *you*… He's ever so charming. He declared himself my loyal subject as soon as I got to Kipper Street. As far as I can tell, he's braver than anyone else around here," she tells me.

Brave is good. I like brave.

"So let's find him!" I say. "Let's go! Where does he live?"

"Well he *might* be at number seven," she says, and my heart drops.

"Fabian? Mean Fabian?"

"What? No, not him," she tuts.

"Who then? Not Mr Dodd? No way!" I'm almost shouting now.

Mr Dodd is Fabian's dad, and he's the headteacher at my school. He's a total stress-head.

"What? No. Neither of those people... You *do* realise I have absolutely *no* idea who they are?"

I'm getting impatient now.

"Your Majesty, does this man have a name?" I ask.

Queen Sardine laughs, "His name's Benny… and he's not a man."

Urgh.

"You mean Benny the cat."

Queen Sardine's eyes light up.

"You know him? Wonderful!"

It really *isn't* wonderful. What good is another cat when we've got a walloping great monster to fight? I hug my knees,

close my eyes and try my absolute hardest to think of a better plan. Anything.

Nothing comes to mind.

"Well, I guess we're going to the Dodds' house then," I mumble.

I drag myself up and start towards the gate, thinking Queen Sardine's going to come too, but she doesn't. Instead, when I turn round, she's acting all fussy, washing and flicking her whiskers.

"Er... Your Majesty? Aren't you coming with me?" I ask.

And she says, "Of course I am! Can't a queen take a few moments to look her best?"

Then she turns her back on me and keeps preening – licking her paws and rubbing them against her brow.

I count to ten and try to keep my cool. We've got a cat to find, a monster to fight, and she's worrying about her looks!

Finally, just when I think we'll be here all morning, she dashes off ahead of me.

"Come on, Ivy!" she says, "Number seven. What are you waiting for?"

BENNY'S ARMY

Benny is a stray. He's a white cat, but you wouldn't know it to look at him because he's normally got dust on his fur from his adventures. He's big and pretty tough (for a cat) and even though he doesn't have owners, he never gets hungry because old Mrs Dodd puts out food and water for him every single day.

She'd let him move in, but Fabian is

allergic to cats. That's what Mrs Dodd says. But she also says Benny probably wouldn't move in anyway, because he's a *free spirit*. Mum says that means he does *what* he wants *when* he wants. Sounds about right.

Queen Sardine starts sniffing the air when we get near number seven.

"*Perfect! We're just in time,*" she whispers.

When we reach the front garden I see what she means. Old Mrs Dodd has just come outside with Benny's food. More stenchy fish.

You can tell Benny's hungry because he's wrapping himself so tightly around

Mrs Dodd's legs so tightly she can hardly walk straight. Unfortunately, Fabian is also outside. He's sitting on the grass with his headphones on, smirking at me.

"Good morning, Mrs Dodd. Hi, F—" I start to say, but he scowls at me and turns away.

"Good morning, Ivy," Mrs Dodd says. "And good morning to you *too*, puss. *Sardine*, isn't it?"

Queen Sardine gives me a look.

"She likes to be called *Queen* Sardine or Your Majesty," I whisper to Mrs Dodd.

"Oh, I beg your pardon, Ma'am. Perhaps Your Majesty would like to share some of Benny's fish?" said Mrs Dodd.

Of course, Queen Sardine loves fish, but with Benny watching, she goes all shy and doesn't want any.

"I think she's a bit nervous," I say.

"Then maybe *you'd* like one? They're quite fresh," says Mrs Dodd, and she holds the little plate of fish right under my nose. "Pilchard?"

Bleh!

"Actually," I say, trying not to be sick, "we were hoping to have a chat with Benny."

Mrs Dodd smiles, "Oh yes, Benny loves a nice chat. I'll leave you to talk in private then," and she puts the dish on the floor, humming as she goes back indoors.

I like Mrs Dodd. She's not like other grown-ups. She talks to Benny like I talk to Queen Sardine. People think she's batty, but she's not.

Right, so now Mrs Dodd's gone, but Fabian's still here, nodding along to his headphones. And Fabian can never resist saying *something* mean.

"Aw, can't you find any *real* friends?" he says. And I can't think of anything clever to say back, so I just roll my eyes like I'm bored (I learned *that* from Queen Sardine). Inside, though, I feel like my tummy's all knotted up. Stupid, mean Fabian.

Anyway, Fabian just smirks, then he

gets up and skulks down the side of the house to the back garden.

I give Benny a stroke and tell him we're there on important business.

"Oh yeah?" he says, not looking up from his pilchards.

"You can talk too, huh?" I say. He ignores me, busy chewing and chomping. But I heard him. I definitely heard him.

I squat down next to him to make sure he's listening.

"Queen Sardine needs your help," I say.

Benny stops chewing and looks at Queen Sardine. He raises an eyebrow. "You need *my* help, Your Majesty?"

Queen Sardine nods shyly.

"Okay, I'm listening," he says. Queen Sardine seems strangely tongue-tied all of a sudden, so *I* tell him all about the enormous, slobbering, stinking monster.

Benny nods seriously. "I've seen it myself," he says, "disgustin' creature. Might be able to sort it out, though... *if* enough of us fight."

Benny counts on his claws, muttering under his breath.

"There's Pudding and Podgekin next door, big Molly from the bungalow, Smudge and Whiskers are always up for trouble, and there's ol' Sausage from Cuttle Street too. Oh, and little Sprout, I s'pose…"

He jumps onto my knee. "That's nine of us altogether. *If* they all agree to fight. Queen Sardine's *new*, see. Not all of 'em reckon she's proper *queen* material. Me, though, I knew soon as I clapped eyes on 'er."

Queen Sardine dips her head, looking all pleased. If cats could blush, I reckon she'd look like a furry tomato right now.

"Anyway," says Benny, "I can probably persuade 'em to fight, just for the fun of it."

Fun? Doesn't sound much like fun to me. "An army of *nine* then," I say, dismayed.

"Ten including you," he purrs.

Ten. Just ten. We'll never sort out a monster with just ten. I close my eyes and sigh. We're doomed.

"*Ha!*" Benny cries. "I know what you're thinkin' — three or four would do — but there's no point taking risks with these things, trust me!" Then he nods to Queen Sardine. "Don't worry, Your Majesty. We'll beat your beast. Mr Trott puts it

in the front garden to do its disgustin'
droppin's every day, before lunch.
This time we'll be waitin'
for it. Won't know
woz' hit it. I'll be
off now, gotta round
up the others. Oh,
and Your Majesty…
I saved you one."

And with a quick
wink, off he goes,
squeezing
t h r o u g h
a gap in
the hedge.

Queen Sardine sniffs the shiny little pilchard and digs straight in. With her mouth full of fish, it's hard to hear what she's saying. But I'm pretty sure she mumbles 'hero' and 'nothing to worry about' a few times.

I'm starting to think my new best friend isn't too smart.

IT'S TIME!

Waiting stinks.

We hang about in my front garden for hours. Queen Sardine sunbathes and I pace up and down. The closer we get to the fight, the more it feels like a really, *really* bad idea. I don't even know *how* to fight. I'll probably just get in the way. Or get eaten.

"You seem a bit uptight," yawns Queen

Sardine. Then she rolls over to sun the other side of her tummy.

A bit uptight? That's it. I explode. **KABOOM!**

"I don't see how *you* can be so calm about this! We're about to fight a monster! One of us might even get—" but I clap my hands over my mouth before the last word slips out.

"Oh, silly Ivy, it's all taken care of. We've got a whole *army* fighting alongside us. Like Benny said, it might even be fun."

"Your Majesty!"

I was *properly* cross then. I don't like seeing anyone get hurt. Even mean people like Fabian. So I don't see how fighting can ever be *fun*.

"Fine. Not fun then… exciting?" she suggests.

I shake my head.

"Well, all right, I suppose it's not really very *queenly* to want to fight, but we might as well make the best of things. Hang on…" Her fluffy brown ears prick up.

She sniffs the air, then grins. "*It's starting! Come on!*" She hisses. She springs onto the fence, fluffs up her fur and dashes off.

I call out for her to wait, but it's too late. My heart thuds and thunks as I swing open the garden gate.

I run out onto the pavement, but where's Queen Sardine? Where are Benny and his army?

The street is calm, silent and empty.

"*Pssssssst! Over here!*"

The voice comes from

Mr and Mrs Trott's garden. I take a deep breath, cross the road and peep over the hedge.

"*Get down,*" hisses Benny, "*and stay that side of the 'edge or you'll give us all away!*"

So I stay where I am, half-offended, but half-relieved. Through a gap in the hedge I can see most of the Trotts' front garden. At first the garden looks empty, but when I look closely I see the cat army, hidden under flowerpots, in bushes, behind garden gnomes. Nine cats in total. All ready to fight. Queen Sardine is hidden behind a big stone donkey.

There are a few impatient mews and meows as the cats wait. Then, all at once, they stop. All ears, eyes and noses point sharply at the front door. Tails swish, fur bristles…

"*It's time,*" hisses Benny. "*The monster is comin'!*"

My heart is now hammering as I watch the front door. I see something move behind the glass. I can hardly breathe. I watch the handle twitch and turn. I shudder as the door groans open. Then out comes...

A puppy.

What?

Sure, it's scruffy, drooly and more like

a big ball of hair than an animal, but this is *definitely* a puppy and not a monster.

I start to laugh, but the cats are still deadly serious, ears flat, tails swishing.

"*Attack!*" bellows Benny.

"No! Wait!" I yell through my gap in the hedge.

They ignore me. They crouch low and wiggle their bottoms, getting ready to pounce!

"He's just a baby!" I cry, running to the gate.

"*Show no mercy to the baby monster!*" yells Benny.

The cats spring forward, yowling, then

slowly start circling the puppy.

"Please stop!" I say. "Can't you see he's *not a monster?*"

Benny looks irritated. "Halt!" he orders. Then he turns to Queen Sardine, "Your Majesty, is your human crazy? Do you still want us to fight this foul beast?"

Queen Sardine is baffled.

"Of course I do," she says.

"*Please!*" I beg her.

She looks from me to
Benny to the puppy, then back
to me, "But Ivy, look at it! It's a ghastly
stinking *monster!*"

"It's just a puppy. A baby *dog.*"

"Surely not… Well, whatever it is, it's a
royal pain in the—"

"*Your Majesty!*" I shout.

"All right, all right! No fighting,"
she tells Benny. "If it is just some
ungroomed hairy lump of a puppy
I suppose there's no point dirtying
our paws on it."

Benny nods, "Your wish is my command, Your Majesty. I'll give the order. Cats, stand down!"

The cats stop. I can tell they're disappointed. One by one, they slink back towards the hedge. Tails soften and bristles become smooth fur again. Podgekin and Sausage lick their paws. The others grumble a bit but all are quick to obey Benny... all but *one*. Sprout.

Little Sprout ignores Benny. He hisses and spits, and swipes a skinny black paw at the enormous pup.

"Sprout! Halt! SPROUUUT!" yells Benny, but Sprout's not listening.

The puppy woofs gleefully at Sprout. He licks Sprout's head. He pushes Sprout over with his big wet nose. Then *he* rolls over too, panting and wagging and **happy, happy, happy!**

But Sprout's *not* happy. He's getting scared. At any moment now, he might get squashed. I've got to help.

I swing open the gate and run into the garden, shouting, "*Stop!*"

But now the puppy thinks I'm playing too. He jumps up and knocks me down, licking my face with a slobbery tongue. Then he barks and bounds back to little Sprout. He lifts his huge front paws into the air, and wobbles there, above the quaking kitten, teetering... tottering... ready to pounce...

PROPER MARVELLOUS

"Enough!"

The order is firm. It's Queen Sardine. The puppy barks and pants but he carefully lowers his paws to the ground.

"Enough," she says again, slinking closer, "and that's quite enough *noise* too."

It's amazing. The puppy is actually listening to her. No more rolling. No more barking.

Queen Sardine sounds brave and calm. There's just the tiniest of nervous wobbles in her tail.

"*Well done, Your Majesty!*" I whisper. "*He's listening! Tell him to sit.*"

Queen Sardine takes a deep breath. "Sit!" she orders.

The pup looks confused.

"Oh for goodness sake!" she sighs. "Sit on your hind legs. Like this…" and she shows him.

The puppy copies her. Unbelievable.

"*Brilliant! Just brilliant!*" I whisper again.

Queen Sardine tiptoes forward a little more. "Now, stay! That means you don't move a muscle until I say so. Understand?"

The pup pants and nods. He sits totally still, next to scared little Sprout.

"That's right," says Queen Sardine, "good monst— good puppy." And she winks at me.

Our eyes are all glued to Queen Sardine as she creeps closer and closer to Sprout.

"All right," she says,

"Sprout's coming with me now. He's not a toy. He doesn't want to play."

The puppy's ears drop. His tail stops wagging.

"Well don't look so sad, you silly beast."

The puppy whimpers.

"Oh, there's no need to be so sensitive!" huffs Queen Sardine.

"Tell him he's a good dog!" I whisper.

Queen Sardine winces. "Oh *really*, this is ridiculous..." she sighs. "There, there. Good dog. Good... *sitting*... and excellent... *staying*... We're all dazzled, I'm sure."

The puppy's tail wags happily again.

Then he gives Queen Sardine an enormous slobbery lick. She shudders in disgust.

"That really isn't necessary," she grumbles. Then she puts her mouth gently on the scruff of Sprout's neck, as cats do, and carries him back to Benny.

Benny bows his head.

"Oh, Your Majesty! That were proper marvellous, that were!" he says, and Queen Sardine goes all bashful.

Benny's army murmurs and mews in agreement, "So brave... Faced the monster... Almost ate her..."

That's not exactly what happened, but I stay quiet, as Queen Sardine looks quite happy with this version of the story.

"All right, all right everyone," I say, "yes, Her Royal Highness is *very* brave but it's time to go now. The puppy needs to do his – er – *business* and…"

Quick as a flash, the cats dash out of the garden, looking disgusted. Queen Sardine goes too. I look at the puppy, still *staying* perfectly still.

"Garden's all yours now, pup!" I say, and leave him to it.

I've got to admit, I'm impressed with Queen Sardine. Even though she's bossy, even though she's vain, she *was* pretty brave standing up to the puppy. None of the other cats went to Sprout's rescue. I'm feeling very proud of my brave best friend right now.

Too bad *I'm* not feeling brave, though, because as we leave the Trotts' front garden, Fabian's out on his bike again, and this time he's got friends with him. I know them both from school. Raji and Sean. They're not *mean* exactly, but

they always laugh when Fabian's being mean, so now my tummy's knotting up again.

"Oi!" yells Fabian.

I stop dead. I want to say something smart, but nothing I could say would do any good.

"Is ickle baby Ivy still wandering about looking for someone to pway wiv?" he shouts.

Raji and Sean start sniggering.

"That flea-bag cat get bored of you?"

Hmph.

I want to be brave and heroic like Queen Sardine. She'd march up to Fabian and put him in his place. But even if I tried, I'd just end up looking stupid. The best I can do is a big fake yawn (got that from Queen Sardine too) and then I keep on walking, back over the road, back to the safety of my front garden.

THE LETTER

"Ivy? Are you all right? That silly human boy really isn't worth worrying about," says Queen Sardine, who's been waiting patiently on my doorstep.

I shrug. "I'm fine," I say, even though I'm not. But I don't want to think about Fabian, so I give Queen Sardine a stroke and tell her she's the bravest cat I know. And she *is*.

"I really put that monster in its place!" she says.

I frown. *Monster* indeed.

"Oh, you know what I mean!" she sighs happily.

"You did do very well with the *puppy,*" I say. "You know, puppies can be trained. You can teach them how to behave. Just takes a bit of work."

Queen Sardine curls herself into a ball in my lap and purrs while I stroke her ears.

I'm so happy just stroking her that I almost can't bring myself to say this next bit — I have to make myself do it.

122

"Your Majesty? I... I think you'll be okay living with the puppy. I think you can train him to be a good dog," I say.

Queen Sardine opens a sleepy eye, "I was thinking the same thing," she murmurs. "It won't be easy but I suppose I'll manage."

Then an idea pings into my head, "Your Majesty…" I say, "maybe I can make it a teeny bit easier for you."

Queen Sardine yawns. "I don't see how, but I suppose if anyone can, *you* can. Go on then, let's hear it."

So, I offer to write a letter for her, telling the Trotts what's what. Queen Sardine thinks it's a good idea, so that's what we do.

Dear Mr and Mrs Trott,

This is Ivy Meadows from across the road. I am writing this for Queen Sardine because she cannot write it for herself. She says that she is not very happy living with the monster puppy. She says that she will put up with him but only if you make a few changes. Mainly, she doesn't like him eating her dinners but there's other stuff too. I will put it all in a list.

1. Puppy must stay away from dinners.
2. Puppy must not ever lick Queen Sardine.
3. Puppy must not sleep in places where Queen Sardine likes to sleep.
4. Puppy must not chase Queen Sardine.

Also, Queen Sardine says you must call her 'Queen Sardine' or 'Your Majesty' or 'Your Royal Highness'.

We hope this is okay. Queen Sardine says she looks forward to living with you properly again and that you are normally very kind people.

Love from Ivy XXX

PS I am giving Queen Sardine my favourite toy called Felina for her to cuddle when she is not happy. Please do not let the puppy eat Felina.

We leave the letter *and* Felina on the Trotts' doorstep. I knock on the door then hide behind the hedge with Queen Sardine. I feel like crying. I bet she'll forget all about me once she's back living with the Trotts and everything's okay again. But I've got do my best to help her — I promised.

Mr Trott opens the door. It's lunchtime and he's got baked-bean juice in his beard and crumbs down his jumper. He's annoyed that no one is at the door.

But then he looks down. He frowns, picks up Felina and the letter, and goes back indoors.

That's that then. We can hear Mr Trott shouting, "Bad Wolfy! Not my beans!"

So *that's* the puppy's name. Wolfy.

"Here goes. Thank you for your assistance, dear Ivy," says Queen Sardine.

I half-smile. It's the best I can manage.

"Wish me luck!" she says, then slinks off down the Trotts' front lawn.

"*Good luck, Your Majesty,*" I whisper.

MR TROTT'S BRILLIANT IDEA

The next day is awful. I get four out of ten in my spelling test at school and at playtime I'm too sad to join in any games.

When school finishes, I walk back home on my own because I don't want to talk to any of my friends. I'm miserable. I miss Queen Sardine, and who knows *when* I'll see her again, now she's back with the smelly old Trotts. I know I'm being mean, calling them that, but I can't help it.

Talking of mean, just as I reach Kipper Street, I hear a **whoosh** of bicycle spokes, and Fabian cuts across me on his bike. I topple, but keep my balance. My heart's thumping and I'm getting those tummy knots again. He laughs, circles round, and does it again, and again, so I'm having to stop, start, stop, start, shuffling down the street. I start to get angry.

We're almost at Fabian's house, then he swerves and screeches right in front of me, so I end up stumbling into his bike.

"Look where you're going, weirdo," he sneers.

That's it. I'm not taking this.

"Fabian   Dodd," I say, "I don't care if *everyone* else thinks you're fantastic, with your bike and your headphones and… and…"

At this point Raji and Sean, who have been cycling behind us, skid to a halt next to Fabian.

I keep going, "… and I don't care if *they* think you're hilarious, *I* know what you *really* are. Mean. *Mean,* mean, *mean!*" I shout.

Fabian slowly reaches up and removes his headphones.

"Sorry, did you say something?" he says, pretending he didn't hear any of it.

Raji and Sean fall about laughing.

I can feel I'm going red in the face. I'm so angry and so embarrassed, and I wish I'd not said anything because it's only made things a million time worse.

But then I see Benny, watching from Fabian's garden, and I see little Sprout,

132

perched on
the gate
to number
nine, looking
at me with his big
green eyes. And, peering out from under
a parked car, there's Queen Sardine.

I remember *I've* got friends too. Good
friends. Why am I bothered about mean
Fabian Dodd and his stupid mates?

Then, because I'm
tired of talking,
I look Fabian
in the eye,

I stick out my tongue and I blow a massive raspberry.

Benny and Queen Sardine both cheer me on with mighty meows, and Sprout makes an excited little **purrrrup** sound. Fabian looks round at his mates and they all start meowing at me too.

They think they're *so* funny.

But I don't care. I hold my head up high and start walking home.

"Poor ickle Ivy," Fabian calls after me. "Pathetic! Run home then, weirdo. Go play with those scraggy cats…"

But then all my Christmasses and birthdays come at once.

"Faaabeeeee!" yells Mrs Dodd.

I whip round and see Fabian's mum running out of the house, calling, "Darling, you *promised* me you wouldn't ride your bike with those darned headphones in. *You promised!* Imagine if something happened to my darling little baby Fabeeee!" And she grabs him in a tight cuddle, fussing over him, while Raji and Sean snigger.

"*Mum!*" Fabian huffs, through gritted teeth.

"I don't care if I'm embarrassing you. You're my precious boy and I won't risk your safety!" she says. "Give me the headphones... Hand them over."

And, as Fabian's face goes bright candyfloss pink, I turn and make my way home.

Queen Sardine soon joins me and we walk side by side.

"Good afternoon, Your Majesty," I say.

"Yes, it is an *extremely* good afternoon," she laughs. "Well done, by the way.

That thing you did with your tongue was extraordinary."

I can't resist smiling. It's my first smile of the day.

"Did your people read my letter?" I ask. "Did they agree to do what we said?"

I do want Queen Sardine to be happy with the Trotts and Wolfy... *Mostly*. But a teeny tiny bit of me wants it to go wrong. That way, she would want to live with *me* again.

"Oh yes! My people took your letter most seriously," she says. "They agreed to all our demands. They really are the most excellent servants."

"Well, that's great… I suppose," I say.

I try to smile again.

"I'd better get inside," I say when we reach my front door.

"Not yet!" she screeches.

Eh?

"Count to twenty, *then* ring the bell," she says. "I've got a surprise for you!"

Then she zips off round the side of the house.

Hmm… Strange. But I do what she says.

"Ivy!" Mum answers the door and gives me a big smiley squeeze. "You're home! Listen, I've had a talk with Mr and Mrs Trott today, and… well, they love how much you care about that cat of theirs and… well, Mr Trott had a *brilliant* idea!"

Mr Trott? He just doesn't seem like the brilliant idea type.

"Ivy, don't pull that face. He's not all bad," chirps Mum. "Seemed quite tickled by some letter you'd sent them. Anyway, aren't you going to ask what his idea was?"

Mum's obviously really excited, so I try to act happy too. Really, I don't believe there's anything that Mum, or Mr Trott or anyone else could do to make things better.

"What was it?" I ask.

"You'll see. It's in the kitchen. Can't miss it!"

I sort-of-smile at Mum politely. Then I go to my bedroom to put away my school bag.

"Oh!" I say.

Queen Sardine's sitting right there, on my bed!

"How did you get in?" I ask, tickling Her Majesty's chin.

Queen Sardine purrs. "Oh, I have my ways," she says, with a knowing smile.

I'm stumped. What's she playing at?

"But I thought… I thought Mr and Mrs Trott were your people again… That's what you said!"

Queen Sardine laughs. "Dear, silly girl! I've told you before, I don't belong to anyone. They *are* my people, but you are *also* my person," she says. "I have decided to let you look after me sometimes, as well as Mr and Mrs Trott. I'll let you give me fish paste and treats, and I'll keep your toes warm on cold nights. I'm a very kind queen. You may stroke me to say thank you."

I don't move. I'm so confused.

"Oh, for goodness sake!" tuts Her Highness, "follow me…"

She leaps off the bed and leads me towards the kitchen.

"But Your Majesty, Mum won't let me leave the bathroom window open any more… so I don't see how you can just visit whenever you feel like it."

Queen Sardine just shakes her head, ignoring my chatter. "Look!" she says.

We step into the kitchen, and I see it

right away. A tiny, shiny, plastic window at the foot of the door. A cat flap!

"Like it?" Mum grins, poking her head around the kitchen door.

I lunge at her with a huge hug. "I love it!" I shout.

"Thought you might," smiles Mum, hugging me back. "Now, I'm just popping out for a couple of minutes. Got to give this back to the

Trotts," she waves a screwdriver in the air. "Get yourself a drink and a biscuit. I won't be long."

I pour some orange squash for me and a saucer of milk for Queen Sardine. I lift her onto the kitchen table (what Mum doesn't know won't hurt her) and I pull up a chair for myself. With a huge grin on my face, I clink Queen Sardine's saucer of milk with my glass.

"Cheers!"

Her Majesty joins in. "Cheers!" she says. "To Mr Trott's brilliant idea!"

THE KIPPER STREET CHORUS

We're just finishing the last slurp of our drinks when Queen Sardine perks up and stares straight at the cat flap. She's heard it first, but now I can too — a chorus of mews, coming from outside.

"Purrrrmission to enter?"

We both recognise the gravelly voice at once. Benny.

"Come in!" we shout at the same time.

And through the cat flap they troop…
Benny, Podgekin, Smudge, Pudding,
Molly, Sausage, Whiskers and, last of all,
little Sprout.

Sprout is dragging something in his
mouth – a small box, tied with a pink
ribbon. The cats sit in a neat line in front
of the kitchen table.

Queen Sardine watches them from on high as they begin to bow and curtsey.

"We've all come to honour our brave 'n' beautiful queen," mews Benny.

"So brave and so beautiful… and so *kind* to forgive those silly Trotts," trill the others.

Queen Sardine nods proudly and leaps down to join them.

Then little Sprout steps forward.

"We have brought you a gift, oh brave, beautiful, kind Queen," squeaks the kitten. He carries the box to Queen Sardine and places it at her feet. "It's to show how we all agree you're a proper queen. Miss Ivy can open it for you, Your Majesty."

I pick up the box and give it a very gentle shake.

"*No!*" hiss all the cats at once.

Jeepers.

"Careful, Miss Ivy," warns Sausage. "It's precious!"

"Sorry," I apologise, as I gently untie the ribbon and open the box. Inside, there's a fragile ring of fishbones, bound

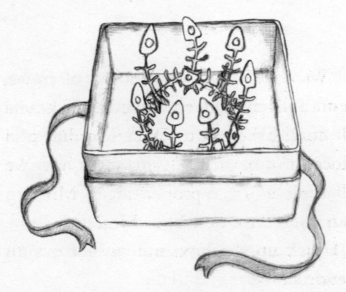

together with thread. "Er... it's... lovely. What is it?"

I hold the strange object at arm's length. It still smells of fish.

Queen Sardine gasps. "A crown! Oh, thank you. Thank you all!"

"Allow me," says Benny. He carefully

lifts the crown with his mouth and places it on Queen Sardine's head. "We saved all the fishbones we could find, and Mrs Dodd 'elped string 'em together," he explains.

Benny swoops down in a low bow. Queen Sardine places a paw on his right shoulder, then on his left.

Then she whispers, "*Sir Benny*," like she's turning him into a knight, right here in my kitchen.

"Cor. *Sir* Benny, eh? Who'da thought it?" He grins, then turns to the others. "Come on you lot, better be off now. It's nearly dinner time!"

And each of the cats bow before leaving through the cat flap, one by one.

When it's just me and Queen Sardine again, I lift her back onto the table. I take a good look at her, purring away, with the fishbone crown balanced on her head.

"It suits you, Your Majesty," I say.

"Yes, I imagine it does," she purrs.

I laugh and tickle her just where she likes it, under her chin.

"It smells of fish, though."

"I know," says Queen Sardine with a royal grin. "It's perfect."

Ivy and Queen Sardine are back
for another fur-frizzling adventure…

coming soon!